Daniel Anctil

Fly Fly

Illustrated by
Corentin Hunter

Midtown Stories for Kids!
Midtown Press

Fly Fly
Copyright © Midtown Press, 2015. All rights reserved.

ISBN 978-0-9881101-6-8

Legal deposit: 1st quarter 2015
Library and Archives Canada

Printed and bound in Canada

Editor: Louis Anctil
Assistant: Daniel Anctil
Design and production: Denis Hunter Design

This book has been typeset in Stempel Schneidler and printed on FSC Flo Dull paper in Montmagny, Quebec in March of two thousand and fifteen by Marquis Book Printing.

Library and Archives Canada Cataloguing in Publication

Anctil, Daniel, 1985-, author

Fly fly / Daniel Anctil ; illustrations by Corentin Hunter.

(Midtown stories for kids)
Poem.
ISBN 978-0-9881101-6-8 (bound)

I. Hunter, Corentin, 1989-, illustrator II. Title.

PS8601.N3355F49 2015   jC811'.6   C2015-901292-9

Fly fly like an eagle
Lord of the sky

Sing sing like the whale
Listen to the orca cry

Fish fish like the bear
Catching from the stream

Swim swim like the dolphin
Cutting through the waves

Look look like a raven
Seeking along the ground

Pace pace like the cougar
Sizing up its prey

Play play like the otter
Floating amidst the kelp

Rise rise like the ducks
Making v's in the sky

Work work like a beaver
Construction is its life

Hunt hunt like a wolf
Running through the land

Watch watch like the owl
Spying through the dark

Flap Flap like the bat
Flying through the night

Sleep sleep little human
Safe from all frights